Shifty McGifty
AND
Slippery Sam

The Cat Burglar

For Dom,
Ian and Len x
T.C.

For Jay
and Holly x
S.L.

First published in 2015 by Nosy Crow Ltd. The Crow's Nest, 10a Lant Street, London SE1 1QR
www.nosycrow.com

ISBN 978 0 85763 482 5 (HB) ISBN 978 0 85763 483 2 (PB)

Nosy Crow and associated logos are trademarks and/or registered trademarks of Nosy Crow Ltd.

Text copyright © Tracey Corderoy 2015

Illustrations copyright © Steven Lenton 2015

The right of Tracey Corderoy to be identified as the author of this work and of Steven Lenton
to be identified as the illustrator of this work has been asserted.

A CIP catalogue record for this book is available from the British Library.

Printed in China by Imago. Papers used by Nosy Crow are made from wood grown in sustainable forests.

1 3 5 7 9 8 6 4 2 (HB) 1 3 5 7 9 8 6 4 2 (PB)

Shifty McGifty
AND SLIPPERY SAM
The Cat Burglar

Tracey Corderoy

Illustrated by
Steven Lenton

There once were two robbers as BAD as could be,
who turned into baker dogs, as you can see.
And now they cook doughnuts so jammy and light,
they're run off their sticky paws
morning till night.

Friends flocked to their café to meet every day,
and share juicy gossip, whilst munching away . . .
"Matilda's had puppies!" cried Duchess.
"Fifteen – nine spotty, five plain
and there's one in-between!"

The Local
Lamp Post
ROBBER DOGS TURN GOOD!

FROM CRIME TO CAKES!

"And what about Rover's
new hairdo?" grinned Fred.
"It looks like a parrot
has perched on his head!"

But suddenly Sam waved his paper about.
"Well, I've got some news, guys!"
he said with a shout . . .

" . . . A robber's in town! She's called Kitty Le Claw.
She's known for disguise and for
breaking the law!

The Local
Lamp Post

**CAT BURGLAR
ON THE LOOSE!**

She's burgled the jeweller's and ten houses, too.
Word's out that the bank is the next job she'll do!"

"Oh, heavens!" shrieked Duchess.
"My bracelets and rings!
The bank's where I keep
all my beautiful things!"

"This calls for a top-secret
meeting!" said Sam.
"With top-secret buns
filled with top-secret jam!"

But Sam had to wait
for his top-secret chat,
for suddenly Dotty exclaimed,
"Look at that!"

A thin little cat – cold as ice – peeped inside.
"I'm Ruby," she shivered, her eyes big and wide.
"I'm looking for work, which is why I've called by."
"Poor thing," whispered Shifty. "Let's give her a try!"

So Ruby was snapped up
to join the boys' team.
She waitressed, she swept,
and her cakes were a dream.

Soon everyone loved her,
she was such a star!
"Oh, Shifty," Sam nodded,
"how lucky we are!"

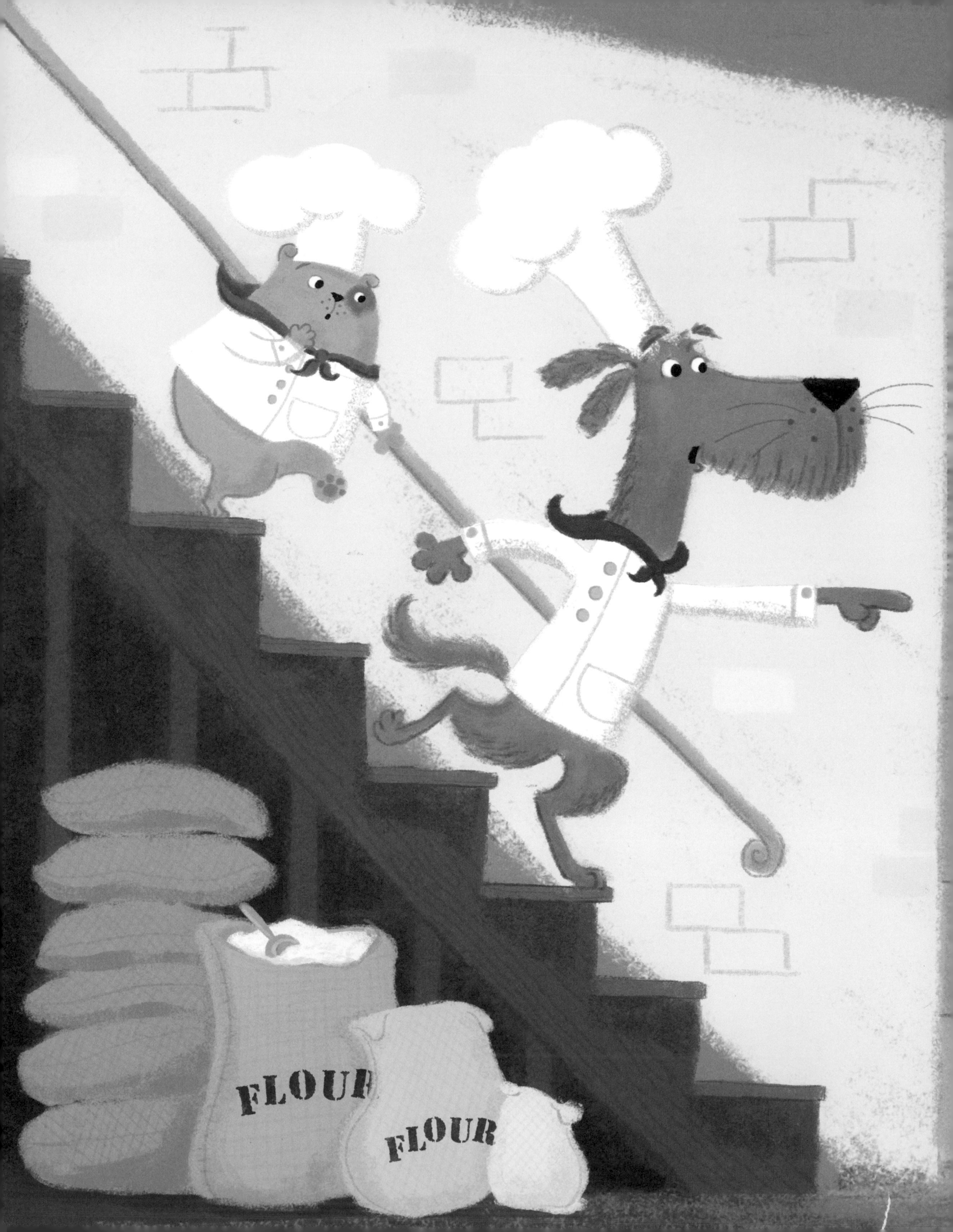
FLOUR
FLOUR

And just after five
when they closed for the day,
the boys found poor Ruby
still sweeping away.

The cellar had never been
so clean before.
"And look!" Shifty pointed.
"She's found an old door!"

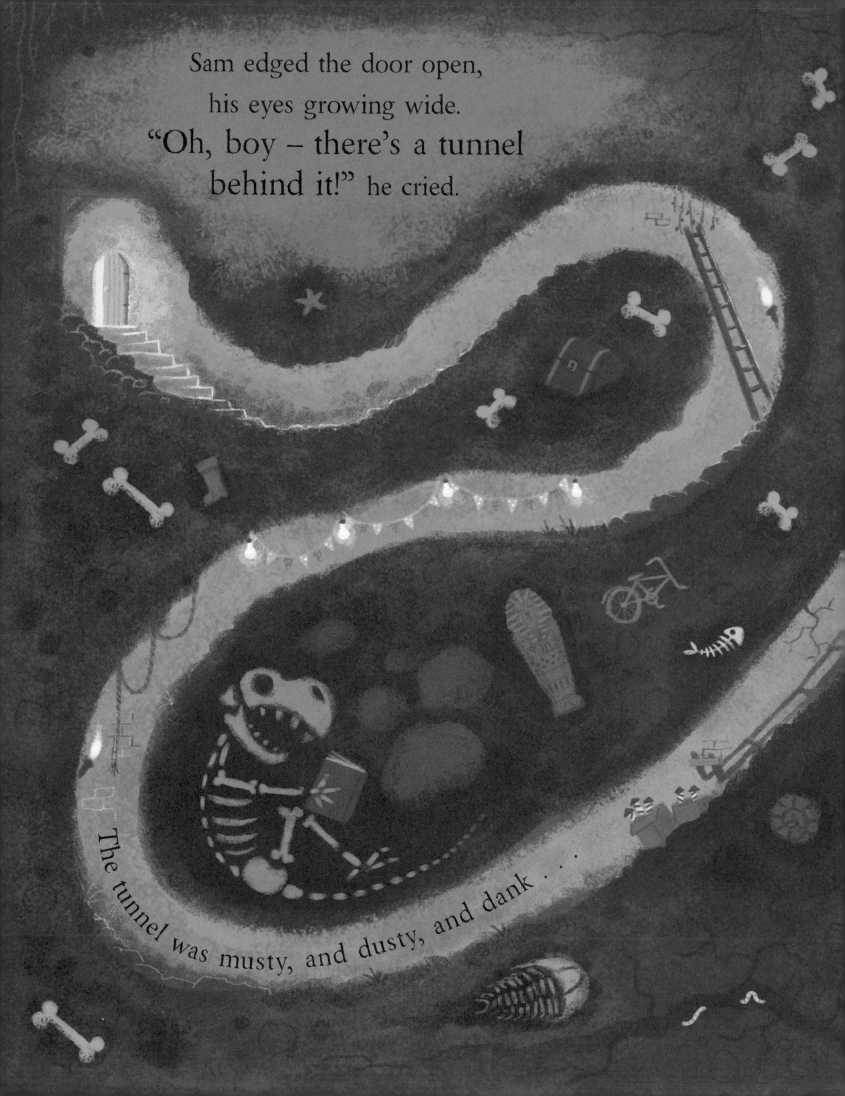

Sam edged the door open,
his eyes growing wide.
"Oh, boy – there's a tunnel
behind it!" he cried.

The tunnel was musty, and dusty, and dank . . . .

. . . And, guess where it led to . . .

BANK
KEEP OUT

. . . Yes! Right to the bank!

The gems in the bank vault were shiny and bright.
Great mountains of diamonds – a robber's delight!
"So twinkly," gasped Shifty, a glint in his eye.
"Just think of the cafés this **treasure** would buy!"

He reached out a paw.
But then Sam shook his head.

"No! Robbing is BAD,
now we're **good** dogs!"
he said.

Back home, tiny stars filled the sky with their light,
as Shifty and Sam baked on into the night.
Then all of a sudden, "Where's Ruby?" Sam said.
"A minute ago she was here baking bread.

Hey – footprints!" he pointed.
"They're Ruby's, I'm sure."
They led down the cellar . . .

. . . then through the old door.

And then through the tunnel, all dusty and dank,
those little white footprints led right to the bank!

The bank guard cried, "Robbers!"
But Shifty squeaked, "Noooo!"
And Sam yelped,
"You've got it all wrong – let us go!"

With that, the REAL robber
raced right past their eyes,
and Ruby threw off her amazing disguise.
Her secret was out now, and everyone saw
that sweet little Ruby was . . .

. . . Kitty Le Claw!

"Ha ha!" shouted Kitty.
"You'll never catch me!"
"We will!" yelled the dogs
as they both wriggled free.

But Kitty was fast as the moon lit her way.

"I fooled you!" she sniggered.
"I tricked you! Hooray!"

She dashed down an alley
and climbed a high wall.
"No, STOP!" Shifty shouted.
"You'll trip and you'll fall."

She raced past the chimneys
and took a great leap, but . . .

"Arrgghh!"
shouted Kitty.
"Too slippy!
Too steep!

Please help me!" she yowled,
clinging on by one paw,
as gems tumbled into
the hands of the law.

"Here, Kitty!"
cried Shifty.
He tossed her his hat.
"A parachute – quick!"
he yelled.
"Grab hold
of that!"

Back down in the alley, Sam had the last word.
"Ha! Gotcha!" he shouted so everyone heard.

And finally Kitty was taken away,
to learn the hard lesson that crime doesn't pay.

Next day in the café,
the town met at four,
to toast the two heroes
with milkshakes galore.

"Oh, boys!" twinkled Duchess. "You stopped that BAD cat!
How totally brave and amazing was that!"
She offered them all of her bracelets and rings.
"No, really," blushed Shifty, "we can't take your things."
"All we need is our little café," beamed Sam . . .

". . . and big, yummy doughnuts with raspberry jam!"